Pete the Cat
The Wheels on the BUS

By James Dean

HARPER
An Imprint of HarperCollinsPublishers

Pete the Cat: The Wheels on the Bus
Copyright © 2013 by James Dean
All rights reserved.

For information address HarperCollins Children's Books, a division of HarperCollins Publishers, 195 Broadway, New York, NY 10007.
www.harpercollinschildrens.com

Library of Congress Cataloging-in-Publication Data
The wheels on the bus / based on the creation of James Dean. — 1st ed.
    p.   cm. — (Pete the cat)
  Summary: Pete the cat's school day is recounted in this twist on the classic song.
   ISBN 978-0-06-219871-6 (hardcover bdg.)
  1. Children's songs, English—United States—Texts. [1. School buses—Songs and music. 2. Schools—Songs and music. 3. Cats—Songs and music.]
I. Dean, James, date.
PZ8.3.W572 2013
782.42—dc23   2012014222
[E]
                                                                   CIP
                                                                     AC

The artist used pen and ink, with watercolor and acrylic paint, on 300lb hot press paper to create the illustrations for this book.

15 16 17 18 SCP 10 9 8 7
❖
First Edition

To my mother and grandfather—Jeanette Brown Thomas and Paul Richard Brown:
Thank you for always being there and making sure we kids had everything we needed.

The wheels on the bus go round and round,
round and round,
round and round.
The wheels on the bus go round and round
all day long.

The horn on the bus goes beep, beep, beep,
beep, beep, beep,
beep, beep, beep.

The horn on the bus goes

beep,

beep,

beep

all day long.

The wipers on the bus go swish, swish, swish,
swish, swish, swish,
swish, swish, swish.

The wipers on the bus go swish, swish, swish all day long.

The signals on the bus go blink, blink, blink,

blink, blink, blink,
blink, blink, blink.

The signals on the bus go blink, blink, blink
all day long.

The motor on the bus goes zoom, zoom, zoom,
zoom, zoom, zoom,
zoom, zoom, zoom.
The motor on the bus goes
zoom, zoom, zoom
all day long.

The door on the bus goes open and shut,
open and shut,
open and shut.

The door on the bus goes

open and shut

all day long.

The kitties on the bus say, "Come on, Pete!
Come on, Pete!
Come on, Pete!"

The kitties on the bus say,
"Come on, Pete!"
all day long.

The driver on the bus says, "Move on back!
Move on back!
Move on back!"

The driver on the bus says,
"Move on back!"
all day long.

Pete's friends on the bus say, "Sit with us!
Sit with us!
Sit with us!"
Pete's friends on the bus say,
all day long.

Sit with us!

LUNCH

The back of the bus bumps up and down,
up and down,
up and down.
The back of the bus bumps up and down
all day long.

The kitties on the bus go

Pete the Cat,

Pete the Cat,

Pete the Cat.

BUS

The kitties on the bus go

Pete the Cat

all day long.

The dog on the bus goes woof woof woof,
woof woof woof,
woof woof woof.

The cats on the bus shout,
"Let's rock out!
Let's rock out!"

The cats on the bus shout,

"Let's rock out!"

all day long.

The wheels on the bus go round and round,
round and round,
round and round.
The wheels on the bus go round and round
All day long.

All day long.

All day long.